Moe McTooth

An Alley Cat's Tale

by Eileen Spinelli

Illustrated by Linda Bronson

CLARION BOOKS · NEW YORK

Clarion Books
a Houghton Mifflin Company imprint
215 Park Avenue South, New York, NY 10003

The illustrations were executed in oil paint.
The text was set in 18-point Bodoni Seventy-Two.

www.houghtonmifflinbooks.com

Printed in Singapore

*Library of Congress
Cataloging-in-Publication Data*

Spinelli, Eileen.
Moe McTooth : an alley cat's tale /
by Eileen Spinelli ; illustrated by Linda Bronson.
p. cm.
Summary: When the weather turned cold and
snowy, the alley cat Moe McTooth was glad
to become an apartment cat, until the
return of spring made him long for
the outdoors.
ISBN 0-618-11760-1 (alk. paper)
[1. Cats—Fiction. 2. Pets—Fiction.
3. City and town life—Fiction.]
I. Bronson, Linda, ill. II. Title.
PZ7.S7566 Mo 2003
[E]—dc21   2002009034

TWP 10 9 8 7 6 5 4 3 2 1

For John McCleary and Barnabas the church cat
—E.S.

For Fin
—L.B.

oe McTooth was an outdoor cat.

By day he prowled Dumpsters and doorways.

By day he napped under the fruit stand.

By day he chased after dockside trucks for sardines that spilled like silver into his mouth.

By night Moe McTooth danced down alleys in the moonlight.

By night on back fences he wailed "The Fishmarket Blues."

By night he stargazed from the tarry roof of the funnel factory.

And life was good.

Then came winter.

By day big wet flakes of snow fell.

By night the wind was so cold that the moonlight creaked.

Slowly, Moe McTooth turned into a hungry fur sack of a cat.

Shivering in doorways. Shuddering on back fences.

One morning, as Moe lay huddled in the stuffing of a junked sofa, a young woman came by.

She stopped. She looked at Moe McTooth. She lifted him into her arms. She took him to her apartment three blocks away.

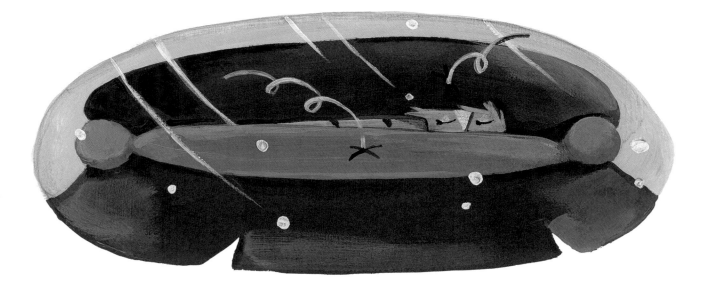

11

There Moe McTooth became an indoor cat.

By day he lapped cream from a blue saucer.

By day he scampered after catnip toys.

By day he napped among geraniums on the windowsill.

By night Moe McTooth curled up in the young woman's lap.

By night he purred in the glow of the fire.

By night he whiskered around the cozy rooms.

And life was good.

And yet . . .

15

There were times when the tree branches scraped against the window in the dappled light.

When the late-night rattle of trucks promised surprises.

When the cold perfume of the outdoors seeped under the locked apartment door.

And Moe McTooth's heart stirred.

17

Spring came.

The air was soft and sweet.

The neighborhood turned willowy green.

Red tulips bloomed.

The young woman opened windows to the new breeze.

She opened the door. Just a crack.

Heart pounding, Moe McTooth slipped out. He scooted up the street.

Half-dressed and barefooted, the young woman tried to catch him.

But Moe McTooth was gone.

All day the woman waited at the window.

All night she kept a small light burning.

But Moe McTooth did not return.

Not that day.

Not the next.

Sadly, the young woman washed the blue saucer.

Sadly, she put the catnip toys away.

And life was lonely.

Out on the streets Moe McTooth prowled the
fruit market. The banana man swatted him with a broom. "Shoo!"
Moe leaped onto a ladder. Purple paint spattered.
He fell asleep in an empty orange crate. Someone dumped him out.
"Sorry, kitty."

23

After several days Moe McTooth became lonely, too.
He missed the young woman. He missed the cozy apartment.
He missed his own blue saucer and catnip toys.

Finally, ear torn, fur matted, Moe McTooth found his way
back to the young woman's doorstep.

She squealed with delight. She lifted him into her arms.
She danced him around the apartment.

Once again, by day Moe McTooth was an indoor cat.

By day he lapped cream from his saucer.

By day he scampered after his catnip toys.

By day he napped among geraniums.

By night, however, Moe McTooth padded out the door into the cool, starry air.

The young woman waved goodbye. "See you in the morning, Moe," she called after him.

*O*ne night the young woman felt a stirring of her own. The sweet darkness of Moe's outdoor world seemed to seep into her heart.

And so, when Moe stepped into the moonlight, the young woman followed.

Together they prowled the shadowy streets.

Together they listened to the silvery music of the outdoor café.

And when the city grew still and quiet, they climbed to the
roof of the apartment building.

Lazily, Moe McTooth gazed up at the stars. The young woman
made dreamy wishes.

Somewhere a distant train whistle sounded.

And life was good.

Together.